To Donald, for bringing budding writers together – M.N.

For Ben – M.P.

Kelpies is an imprint of Floris Books
First published in 2018 by Floris Books

The publisher acknowledges subsidy from
Creative Scotland towards the publication
of this volume

Also available as an eBook

British Library CIP data available
ISBN 978-178250-365-1
Printed & bound by MBM Print SCS Ltd, Glasgow

and the Case of the
Vanishing Viking

Written by Mike Nicholson
Illustrated by Mike Phillips

Leabharlanna Poiblí Chathair Baile Átha Cliath
Dublin City Public Libraries

THE SQUAD

Kennedy

Nabster

Laurie

Colin the hamster

Mrs Gomez

Astrid and Erik

Alistair and Rab

The Vanished Viking

ALL ABOUT LONGSHIPS

Longships were one of the Vikings' greatest inventions and allowed them to travel as far as Asia, Africa and even America. Light and quick, they could be sailed on rivers and oceans, and could even be picked up and carried!

Steerboard
Wooden board used for steering, fastened to the right-hand side of the ship.

Oars
Used on rivers, or when there was no wind for the sail.

DID YOU KNOW...
In good conditions, longships could travel up to 17 mph.

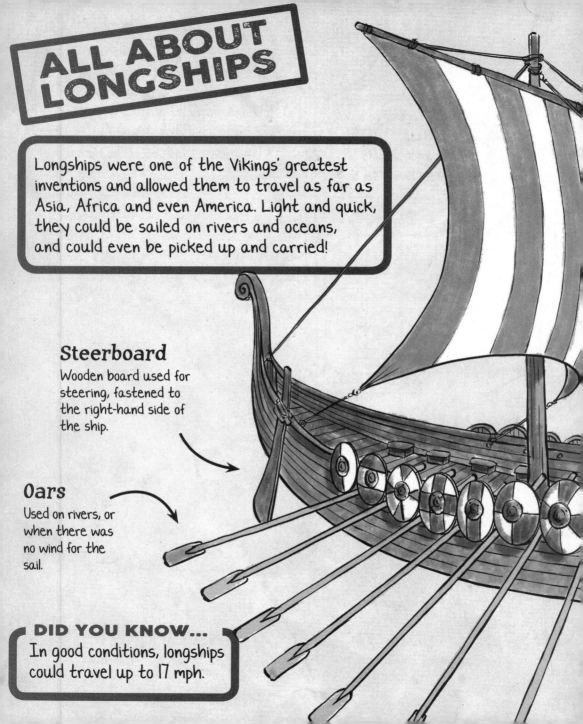

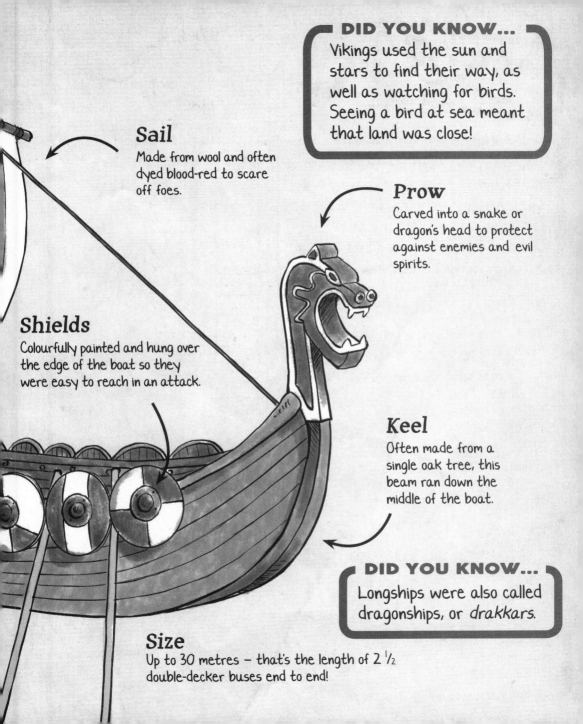

Sail
Made from wool and often dyed blood-red to scare off foes.

Prow
Carved into a snake or dragon's head to protect against enemies and evil spirits.

Shields
Colourfully painted and hung over the edge of the boat so they were easy to reach in an attack.

Keel
Often made from a single oak tree, this beam ran down the middle of the boat.

Size
Up to 30 metres – that's the length of 2 ½ double-decker buses end to end!

Some people think that museums are boring places.

Glass cases. Old stuff. Dust.

Wrong.

Think more of

wild animals

ANCIENT MUMMIES

enormous insects

COLOURFUL COSTUMES

glittering treasure

and amazing objects found nowhere else in the world.

Then imagine that each thing in the museum has its own strange story. With secrets from the past to be uncovered. Codes to be cracked. Odd characters and their fiendish plans. Each one creating a job for a team of expert investigators:

In this book you will find the Squad in the depths of the museum, somewhere in a maze of corridors and stairs.

Today, like every day, they have a puzzle to solve...

Chapter 1
In which disappearing
doesn't happen and then does

Nabster was frowning deeply. The Museum Mystery Squad's technical expert glanced at an open booklet propped on the table in the Squad's headquarters. His hands hovered over three upside-down cups in front of him.

"Keep your eye on the cup you think is covering the ball," he instructed Kennedy. She leaned in, her frizzy ginger hair spilling onto the table. "Right," said Nabster, "here goes!" He moved the cups around each other in rapid figures of eight, then looked back at the magic set booklet he had been reading.

"OK, you will be AMAZED by my ASTONISHING power to make a solid object DISAPPEAR! Which cup do you *think* the ball is under?"

"Easy." Kennedy tapped the middle cup.

Nabster lifted it.

A little red ball sat underneath.

"Aaaw!!" Nabster groaned in annoyance as he stacked up the cups. "What am I doing wrong?"

"Sounds like making things disappear takes lots of practice," said a voice from the sofa.

"Well you should know," said Kennedy. "Laurie Lennox – the Invisible Man!"

It was true. Laurie was in his usual position in the

Squad HQ: burrowed out of sight in his sleeping bag, invisible to the untrained eye. When he was awake and upright, spotting Laurie was much easier, because he was always wearing a wacky but somehow stylish combination of clothes chosen from his overflowing wardrobe rail. Yesterday he'd been dressed in lime green from head (hat) to middle (waistcoat) to toe (shoes). He'd looked like a lanky lizard with big glasses all set for the catwalk.

"Keep practising!" said Kennedy cheerfully to Nabster. "Ask me again, when you're ready. Soon, hopefully, because there's not much else to do." She flicked through her diary, but the Museum Mystery Squad had no case to solve, so there was nothing to write about.

Kennedy Kerr was actually quite good at her own form of disappearing trick. When there was something to investigate, she took off like a shot, sprinting through the museum's corridors. She was so speedy *and* quick-thinking that no one could keep up with her.

Mohammed McNab, otherwise known as Nabster, was also able to vanish – into his own tech-filled world, where he could be lost for days, connecting wires or tightening bolts. His latest creation was a tracking device, allowing him to clip a tracker to any person or thing, then follow its movements on a hand-held screen. He'd made it to help find his favourite screwdriver, which always seemed to be missing when he needed it.

As the Squad had no investigation on the go, Nabster was trying, for a change, to figure out how magic works. His magic kit included playing cards, mirrors, boxes with secret moving sides and a wand that changed length. He planned to start small and work his way up. His ultimate aim was to make Colin the hamster disappear, but right now even the ball-and-cup trick was proving too difficult.

You could say that Colin had already *kind of* disappeared. The cage in the corner of the Squad HQ seemed full of straw and not much else, but if you peered closely you would see the slow rise and fall of the hamster's bedding. Underneath, the Museum Mystery Squad's smallest member was asleep, worn out by a busy morning eating carrots.

Laurie disappeared   Colin disappeared   Ball NOT disappeared

A sound from the laptop distracted Nabster from his failed magic trick.

Kennedy darted round to look. The sleeping bag on the sofa began to stir, and even Colin emerged from his cosy nest.

It was an email from Magda Gaskar, the Museum Director. "Looks like there's been a real disappearance," said Nabster as he read.

I need to find out what's happened. Can you please investigate?

Kind regards,

Magda Gaskar

Museum Director

Nabster opened the attached photo on the HQ's big smartboard screen.

"Woah!" Laurie jumped.

The large Viking figure looked rather fierce and wielded a double-sided axe.

Colin gave a squeak and dived beneath his straw.

"How can a life-size exhibit have disappeared?" Laurie pondered. As well as snoozing, asking questions was one of his greatest talents.

"Perhaps by magic?" Kennedy grinned at Nabster.

"Well, we know that's harder than it seems," said Laurie. "But really, how are we going to look for something that's vanished?"

"Go wherever it was last seen," replied Kennedy, "and search for any clues that might have been left behind."

"Viking Zone!" said the three Squad members together.

Nabster pushed the laptop aside and gathered equipment he thought might be helpful for finding missing things:

• a magnifying glass (for looking close up)

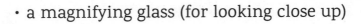
• binoculars (for looking far away)

• fingerprint powder (to see

anything unseen)

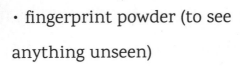

• a torch (to throw light on

anything mysterious)

• his camera (for seeing the

same things again later)

• his Scanray (because he never

went anywhere without it)

• the usual collection of random bits of string,

wire, keyrings, buttons,

paper clips (because you just never

know when you might need them)

• and his trusty screwdriver (because his new tracking device had helped him locate it under Laurie's sofa, and he was determined to use it for something).

Meanwhile, Laurie was flicking through outfits on his wardrobe rail.

"Mmmm... Vikings... Vikings... let's see... too dark... too bright... wrong shade of pineapple... oh... now *that* would be perfect!"

Two minutes later he was ready. He'd found a metal helmet and a big woven cloak, which he pulled together with a large brooch and pin. Underneath he wore a tunic with a thick belt, and leather slippers. He looked every inch the Viking, except that he'd also chosen to lift the mood with a bow tie.

Nabster laughed. "You look like a Viking heading to a posh restaurant."

"Hmmm. I don't think they had the right table manners for fine dining," replied Laurie.

Viking dining styles

Kennedy was long gone. While Nabster and Laurie were getting ready, she was already darting through corridors and upstairs to the museum's exhibition rooms.

"It's a bit odd, going to look at something that's not there," said Laurie, leaving the HQ.

"Well," said Nabster, "sometimes we can find ways of seeing things that aren't right in front of us. Look!"

He held up the screen of his new tracking device. It showed a flashing dot speeding through a maze of lines.

"What's that?" asked Laurie.

"Kennedy," replied Nabster, smiling. "I popped the tracker in her pocket earlier. She's gone, but with this she's still visible. See! She's nearly at the Viking Zone!"

Nabster's gadget *was* very clever, but it couldn't show what was waiting for their fast-running friend: something looming high over her, with monstrous red eyes, sharp teeth and a long tongue.

Chapter 2
In which there are
skull-splitters and leg-biters

Nabster and Laurie arrived at the Viking Zone to find Kennedy staring up into the gaping mouth of a dragon. Though its eyes were fierce, they were fixed and unseeing, and this dragon had no body or wings. Instead, the creature's neck curved to form the prow of a wooden Viking longship.

The replica longship was enormous, dominating the large exhibition space. Colourful shields lined each side of it, and below them a row of oars poked out.

"I'm glad that's not a real dragon," said Laurie, looking up at its carved fangs.

"Imagine standing on a beach and seeing that thing appear and a bunch of Vikings jump out," said Nabster.

"Like that guy!" Kennedy pointed to a nearby model. The figure had a huge beard, crazy eyes and was biting the edge of his shield. He was wearing an enormous bearskin as a cloak.

"It says he's a berserker." Nabster read the model's information panel. "One of the wildest Viking warriors."

"Vikings are like savage pirates," said Kennedy.

Laurie looked around at the displays of Viking farming and home life. "Seems there's more to them than that."

Proving his point, a large sign introduced the Zone to visitors:

≈ THE VIKINGS ≈
RAIDERS, TRADERS AND SETTLERS

"No mention of them vanishing, though," Laurie continued. "OK, so how could a Viking leave this room?"

"Well, there's only one exit for visitors." Nabster pointed at the wide doorway they'd just walked through. It led to the museum's main hall. "At the back there's a **STAFF ONLY** door but that just goes to a stairwell. It couldn't be hoisted out through the ceiling: there are three more levels of the museum above this one."

"Surely a Viking heading out that main door would have been spotted," said Kennedy. "There are always people in the main hall and the café."

"Maybe he popped out there to find something tasty," joked Laurie. He was beside a display about Viking food. "It says here that Vikings ate seagulls, horses, seals and whales!"

"*I'd* vanish if that was on the menu!" said Nabster.

"Plus bread, berries, nuts and fish," Kennedy read. "That sounds a lot better. I don't think food is involved in the vanishing."

"Here's some information on why the Vikings travelled," said Nabster. "This might tell us something about where a Viking would disappear to." He was in the Traders section next to a set of scales where museum visitors could balance silver objects with different Viking weights. "It says Vikings journeyed to buy and sell things. They sold their fish, fur and wool for stuff like silk and silver from faraway places."

"Do you think someone has swapped or traded our missing Viking?" asked Laurie.

"Unlikely," replied Kennedy. "We need to examine the spot it disappeared from. To the longship!"

The Squad trooped up the ramp and into the replica ship.

They were met by a display of wicked-looking weapons, including axes, spears and swords. Some had names like 'Leg Biter' and 'Skull Splitter'. Beyond this were low wooden boxes arranged in lines.

These sea chests kept Vikings' belongings safe, and also acted as seats for those rowing the huge boat. Before the Squad could look any further, they were interrupted by a familiar voice.

"Ahoy there!" The cheery face of Gus the security guard came up the ramp behind them. "I see everything on board is going cheap!"

Kennedy, Nabster and Laurie all looked blank.

Gus grinned. "Because there's a big *sail*! Get it?... Big sail? Like a *sale* in a shop, so, cheap..."

There was a pained silence.

"Yeah, we get it, Gus," said Kennedy, unable to raise a smile at his terrible joke. As the museum's security guard, Gus was hugely helpful to the Squad. He was like an extra pair of eyes and ears around the building, but there was a catch. A very big catch. Listening to Gus's jokes was often the most difficult part of any investigation.

Even Kennedy wasn't fast enough to stop Gus cracking another one.

"I suppose you're here to *axe* some tricky questions?" Gus stood beside the weapon labelled

'Skull Splitter'. "Axe questions... get it?... *Ask* questions?"

"Who needs an axe?" muttered Laurie. "Gus's jokes *always* split my skull!"

Kennedy was quicker this time. "So, Gus, what do you know about this vanishing Viking?"

A new voice answered instead: "He was standing right over there until yesterday morning." It was Magda Gaskar the Museum Director, stepping on board and pointing to a space at the far end of the longship. They walked over to inspect the gap left by the missing model. Next to the space was a beautifully carved wooden sledge piled high with shiny objects.

"Treasure!" Laurie peered closely at metal pots full of silver coins, beads and bracelets, and brooches that looked like silver wolves, dragons and snakes.

"I don't get it." Nabster stared at the treasure and the gap beside it. "A fake figure made of fibreglass disappears while real Viking silver stays put..."

"Any of this treasure would be easier to move," said Laurie. "You couldn't carry a huge Viking model without a struggle. You'd need a wheelbarrow!"

"Well, none of the staff reported seeing anything like that," said Gus.

"It's very odd." Magda nodded. "That's why I've put you on the case."

"Remind us what our missing man was wearing?" asked Laurie.

"He was dressed a bit like me!" Someone completely unexpected stepped on board and joined the conversation.

"Wow, here's a Viking who's definitely not in any danger of vanishing," murmured Nabster. He was right. This real, live Viking was *huge*. Wearing a helmet that tamed some (but not much) of his wild fair hair, he had a beard enormous enough for a family of finches to nest in. A cloak of animal skins draped over his sleeveless top helped show off his boulder shoulders and tree-trunk arms, which were covered in bracelets and tattoos.

"Great outfit!" whispered Laurie.

His jewellery collection was impressive too. Not only was he wearing a hefty silver medallion on a leather string, he sported a nose ring, eyebrow ring and multiple earrings.

"Ah, yes," said Magda, smiling. "I should introduce you

35

to Erik, one of our Viking educators from Norway. He talks to school groups. Usually he's with his twin, Astrid, who also looks the part..." Magda glanced towards the longship entrance, but there was no sign of a second Viking stepping aboard.

"She'll be here later," said Erik. "I was so sad to hear our Viking Captain is missing. Normally he stands here while school groups sit on the sea chests and imagine they are rowing across oceans, like the Vikings."

Kennedy nodded but turned her attention to her plan of action, determined not to be distracted by all these arrivals. "OK, look for clues," she said to the Squad. "First where the Viking stood, then in the rest of the longship."

"What sort of clues?" asked Laurie.

"Anything. The figure would have been heavy to move – check the floor for scuff marks, and keep your eyes peeled for anything strange."

Nabster began measuring the space where the figure had been, while Kennedy and Laurie peered around the sledge of treasure and between the oars. As they searched, some schoolchildren wandered onto the longship. One of them bumped into a sea chest and a flash of white caught Laurie's eye. He stared hard through his big glasses as it rolled across the wooden hull.

Reaching down, he picked up the small, round object. There was a gasp from one of the schoolchildren before another let out an ear-splitting scream.

Laurie was holding an eyeball.

Chapter 3
In which pranks are a possibility

It was chaos! The schoolchildren panicked and started to cry, until a teacher appeared and calmed them down. Nabster helped by using his favourite gadget, the Scanray, to confirm that the eyeball was fake and made of

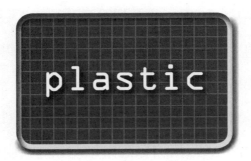

plastic

After careful examination, Erik said he recognised the pale-blue eye as being from the missing Viking figure.

"You did tell us to keep our eyes peeled," said Laurie to Kennedy.

Gus grinned, and immediately asked: "Can I give you a *hand* looking for other body parts? I'd like to help you get *a-head* in this case..."

But despite the promising start, further searching revealed no more pieces of Viking. The Squad decided to return downstairs – with (after Magda gave permission) a new companion from the Viking Zone.

Using a porter's trolley, Gus loaded up the shield-biting berserker Viking. He wheeled it through corridors and bumped it gently downstairs to the Squad HQ.

"Having our own Viking figure will mean we can experiment," said Kennedy. "Like, just how *does* a Viking lose an eye?"

"Maybe I can make this one vanish too." Nabster was eager to try more magic.

Colin didn't look very sure about the fearsome new arrival and scurried back into the safety of his straw.

Gus slid the berserker onto the floor, saying, "Look! I think he might be even crazier now. He's completely off his trolley! ... Get it?...'Off his trolley' means a bit crazy."

The Squad ushered Gus out of the room before he produced any more punishing punchlines, then began their (not very scientific) experiment.

"Let's see whether the eyeball is loose or rolls out," said Kennedy.

Laurie tapped the Viking's head and shook the figure by the shoulders. There was a bit of rattling but the model remained in one piece. Then Kennedy and Nabster lifted it by the head and feet and held it out flat. Everything seemed OK until...

CRASH!

The berserker's head came off in Kennedy's hands and the body smashed onto the floor.

"Oops...!" said Kennedy and Nabster together.

Laurie looked worried. "I promised Magda we'd look after Mr Berserker here!"

"We'd better try and fix it." Kennedy rested the head

on the desk, helping Nabster get the body back onto
its feet.

THUMP!

The head rolled off the desk onto the floor.

"Oops again!" said Kennedy.

"Nooo!" Laurie imagined Magda watching them.

"Look!" Nabster pointed. "Its eye has fallen out!"

Sure enough, a plastic eyeball rolled across the floor.

"A-ha!" said Laurie. "Do you think the missing Viking also fell heavily? Maybe that's how it lost an eye."

Kennedy picked up the new eyeball. "Maybe. But how does that connect to the figure vanishing?"

"Not sure," admitted Laurie. "Can we fix this one?"

Nabster managed to pop the berserker Viking's eyeball back in and, with a bit of screwdriver assistance, he reattached the head.

Kennedy turned to the smartboard, pen in hand. "OK, let's brainstorm. We've got a sense of how the eyeball came loose: the figure was knocked hard or tipped over. But why would anyone play around with a Viking figure in the first place?"

"Fancy dress?" suggested Laurie. "Maybe they needed a costume."

Nabster grinned. "Well, if someone stole its clothes then there's a naked Viking figure somewhere!"

"OK, maybe they were just mucking about," Laurie continued. "What if a prankster hid behind the figure to give a friend a fright – for a laugh. It might have got knocked over."

"Or another kind of prank," suggested Kennedy. "It could have been moved somewhere daft for fun, like up on the roof or into the lift, or outside standing in a queue for the bus!"

"But the big question remains," said Laurie. "How did the Viking move anywhere without being seen? It's not in the room, so how did it get out? Gus said staff saw nothing suspicious. But if you dragged a Viking figure around, you'd quickly have an audience."

"So it must have happened at night when no one was here!" Kennedy concluded.

"But even then it would be seen," said Nabster.

"By who?" asked Laurie.

"Not by a person," said Nabster. "Think gadget."

"CCTV?" suggested Kennedy.

Nabster nodded. "Exactly. There are cameras in different parts of the museum and at the exits. Maybe one recorded a Viking on the move."

They soon had a plan. Laurie and Nabster would

split up and search the zones reached by the staff stairwell at the back of the Viking Zone. If the Viking figure was still in the museum, it was about to be found.

Meanwhile Kennedy would go through CCTV footage with Gus to see if they could catch a Viking in the act of vanishing.

Chapter 4
In which Mrs Gomez
wants to **WIN**

The Squad headed upstairs and popped into the Viking Zone before beginning their separate missions. As soon as they stepped through the entrance, they could hear Erik's voice inside the longship. They found him answering questions from schoolchildren, who were sitting on the wooden sea chests. There was still no sign of his twin.

"Was this boat fast?" a girl asked.

"Really speedy," said Erik. "It was designed to move quickly, powered by thirty-two people all rowing hard!"

"Why is there a skeleton behind you?" A boy pointed at a glass box containing ancient bones.

"Ah! One of my ancestors!" said Erik. "When important Vikings died, longships were used for burials. Instead of a coffin, a whole ship was buried with the body on board. The skeleton here was found in a burial ship along with all of this treasure." He pointed to the decorated wooden sledge with its weapons and jewels.

CLAP-CLAP-CLAP-CLAP-CLAP

Erik was interrupted by loud clapping that echoed round the longship. It came from the class teacher.

"OK children!" she shouted. "We have one hour. Keep looking around, and gather as many other ideas as you can.

Remember, it's the inter-class competition for the best display in school. And what are we going to do?"

There was silence from the class. One boy put his hands over his ears like he knew what was coming.

"WE'RE GONNA WIN!!!!" roared the teacher, her clenched fists punching the air.

The Squad froze in shock. Erik was bewildered, but the class looked like they had seen it all before.

"Mrs Gomez... isn't it the taking part, not the winning, that counts?" asked a small girl quietly.

The teacher slowly turned around to locate where the question had come from.

"Yes, of course," she said in a soft voice. "But the reason we take part is... **SO WE CAN WIN!!**" Her eyebrows looked like they might take off as her face strained with the effort of her battle cry.

"Can we take this stuff back to school, Miss?" A boy pointed to the sledge of treasure. "Then we'd definitely win!"

"Only if no one's looking," said Mrs Gomez, sounding half-serious and fully scary. "You're right! If we had

some real Viking objects, victory would be **OURS!"**
She laughed like a supervillain in a movie.

"I think she might be more berserk than the berserker," muttered Nabster.

As the school group moved off, the Squad watched Mrs Gomez approach Erik. "Can I be *very* cheeky and ask whether there's anything we could take for our display?" Her question managed to sound both friendly and threatening at the same time.

Erik rustled around in his bag, keen to keep the teacher happy.

"Can we go?" asked Laurie. "If Mrs Gomez gets her hands on a Skull Splitter, things could get messy!"

The Squad went their separate ways as planned. Nabster visited the best places for pranking people with a Viking model. He snooped behind doors, checked in cleaning cupboards and toilet cubicles, looked in the lift, and climbed stairs to peek on the roof. He found no Viking lurking anywhere unusual. He sped up as he

passed Mrs Gomez at the cloakroom checking in two long cardboard tubes. The cloakroom attendant looked a little terrified and Nabster guessed the teacher might just have shared her vision for **VICTORY!**

Laurie checked the staff stairwell at the back of the Viking Zone, and the rooms that came off it, in case the Viking had been dragged upstairs into a different zone for fun. He made sure that the vanishing Viking wasn't now riding a woolly mammoth, driving a Victorian steam engine, or hiding inside a spacesuit.

Finally, he examined the remaining figures in the Viking Zone. Back on the longship something caught his eye, sticking out from behind the skeleton's display case. It was a torn piece of paper titled **A Bit of Viking Fun** and covered in rows of strange twig-like symbols in neat order. It looked like code.

"A bit of Viking fun?" he thought, pocketing the piece of paper. "I wonder if this is anything to do with the pranksters?"

As he left the room, he nearly bumped into Mrs Gomez, who was struggling past carrying a bulging bag in both arms.

"No pain... no gain!" she urged herself on.

Meanwhile, Kennedy was with Gus looking at CCTV footage from the night the Viking disappeared.

"This could take a while." Gus sounded unusually gloomy about the size of the job. There were no cameras in the Viking Zone itself, but there was one on the door to the museum's main hall. He was now looking at all the images it had recorded that night. While he worked, Kennedy watched rows of screens, all showing what was going on inside the museum. She spotted Nabster and Laurie checking cupboards and exhibits, as well as Mrs Gomez carrying a large cardboard box.

Gus found no sign of Vikings on the move in the night-time footage, so Kennedy left him checking the daytime CCTV, and hoped that Nabster and Laurie's searches had turned up something useful.

Back in the HQ, Kennedy said, "You know, if you give Gus a big job to concentrate on, he stops telling bad jokes."

Nabster's information was less useful. "I opened thirty-two doors. Nothing odd behind any of them."

Laurie's search had been equally fruitless. "Although I did find this," he said, pulling out the scrap of paper.

"Looks like secret writing," commented Nabster, scanning the strange symbols.

"I thought **A Bit of Viking Fun** could be some kind of note from one prankster to another," said Laurie. "Maybe if we solve the code it will lead us to the vanished Viking!"

They all studied it, but without a key to the symbols it made no sense at all.

A Bit of Viking Fun

F ᛒᚠᛉ ᚱᛟᛈᛗᚱ
ᛒᛁᚠᛅᛗᛋ ᛏᚢᛗ
ᛟᚠᚱᛋ

ᛉᛟᚢ ᛈᛁᛚᛚ

"So, this eyeball is still all
we have," said Nabster, moving
it around under his magic cups
on the tabletop. "We've checked
every possible escape route from
the Zone and the night-time
cameras, and we still have no
idea how the big Viking figure vanished."

"Maybe we should think smaller," said Laurie,
resting on the sofa after his tiring mission. "What if
pranksters broke the figure up? If there's an eyeball,
maybe there are other pieces too."

Kennedy nodded. "You're right! Moving or hiding
something life-size seems impossible. Smaller bits
would be much easier."

"Then pieces of Viking could be smuggled out of the museum in containers," said Nabster.

"I saw Mrs Gomez carrying a box," remembered Kennedy. "Something like that?"

"I saw her too," said Laurie. "But it wasn't a box, it was a bag."

"It wasn't a box *or* a bag," chipped in Nabster. "It was two long tubes."

Laurie sat up. The Squad members stared at each other. They had all seen Mrs Gomez in different places, at different times, carrying different items.

"She's desperate to win the display competition," said Kennedy.

"A life-size figure would look really impressive in a classroom," Nabster agreed.

Laurie thought about seeing Mrs Gomez at the cloakroom. "If she came in yesterday, before the school visit, and hid the Viking pieces, she could be picking them up now, hidden in boxes and bags. Then she could reassemble them back at school and **WIN WIN WIN!**"

"Cardboard tubes with Viking arms inside!" said Nabster.

"A box for a head with a helmet!" cried Kennedy.

"A bag for a body!" finished Laurie.

Nabster picked up the Viking eyeball and waved it. "We need to keep a close eye on Mrs Gomez!"

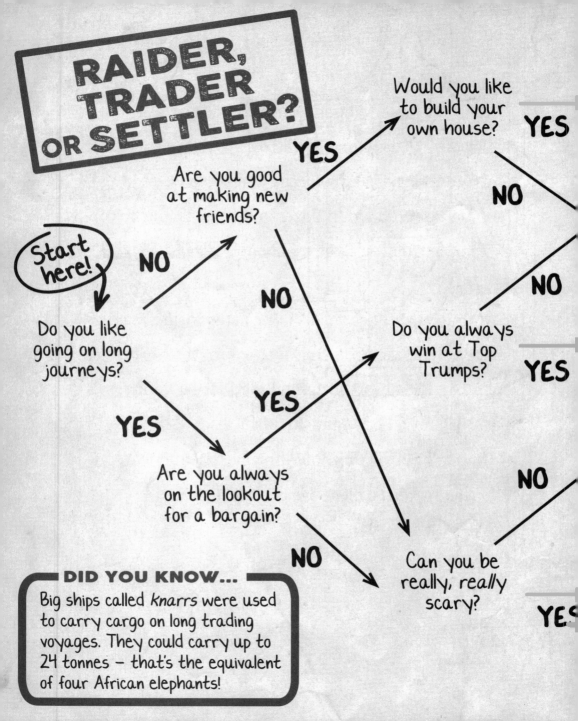

RAIDER, TRADER OR SETTLER?

Start here!

Do you like going on long journeys?

NO → Are you good at making new friends?

YES → Are you always on the lookout for a bargain?

Are you good at making new friends?

YES → Would you like to build your own house?

NO →

Would you like to build your own house?

YES

NO

Do you always win at Top Trumps?

NO

YES

Are you always on the lookout for a bargain?

YES → Do you always win at Top Trumps?

NO → Can you be really, really scary?

Can you be really, really scary?

NO

YES

DID YOU KNOW...

Big ships called *knarrs* were used to carry cargo on long trading voyages. They could carry up to 24 tonnes — that's the equivalent of four African elephants!

Do you like looking after animals?

YES → You'd be a **SETTLER**

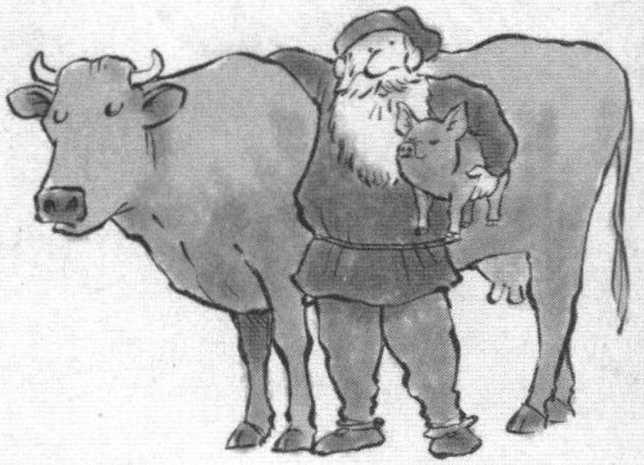

NO ↓

Do you like collecting things?

YES → You'd be a **TRADER**

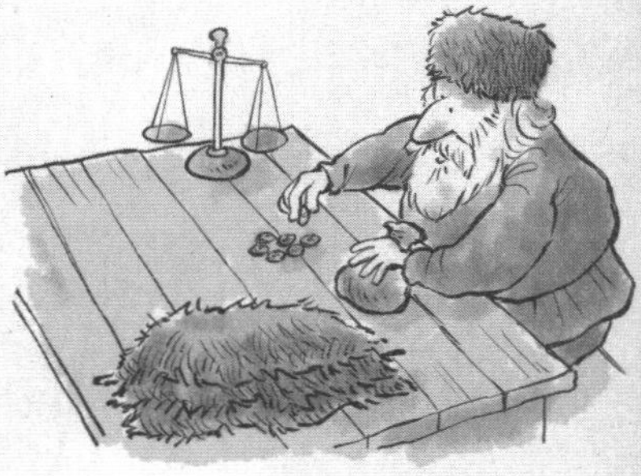

NO ↓

Have you ever raided the biscuit tin without asking first?

YES → You'd be a **RAIDER**

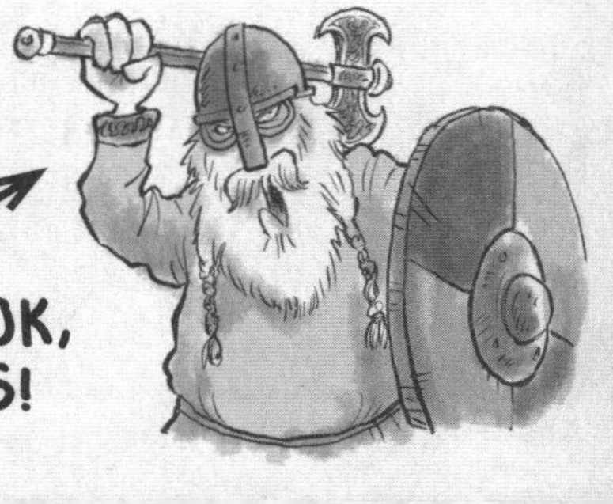

NO → Really? Are you sure? → **OH, OK, YES!**

Chapter 5
In which there are crunching footsteps

"Colin is quiet today," said Laurie as they prepared to leave the Squad HQ.

"He's been hiding ever since that berserker arrived," observed Kennedy.

"Maybe he'd be happier coming with us rather than being left alone with it?" said Nabster, lifting the hamster out of the cage. He filled a side pocket of his equipment bag with straw and half a carrot, and Colin nestled down for a rare trip outside the HQ.

Upstairs, as they made their way across the entrance hall, the Squad were met by the familiar face of Bea Menzies, the museum's cleaner.

"Busy day, Bea?" asked Laurie.

"Hmph. Every day is busy just now!" She sounded harassed. "There are roadworks going on outside and every single visitor is coming in with *filthy* shoes. This grit is never-ending!"

"I see what you mean," said Nabster, his foot crunching on the usually smooth marble floor.

Bea shot a disapproving look towards two men in neon-yellow jackets who had stepped through the front door.

"It's their fault," she said under her breath. "That big man is in charge of the work."

The bulky man and his equally bulky boots left a grittier trail than every other visitor. Removing his hard hat and wiping his forehead with a handkerchief, the man spotted that he and his workmate were being stared at – or rather their boots were. He looked a bit embarrassed as he made his way towards Bea and the Squad.

"Sorry about all this!" he apologised. "I'm afraid you'll have to put up with a couple more days of mess. We're putting in new streetlights and paving outside. But I promise you the pavement will be as well-lit and smooth as this marble floor when we're done!"

The man introduced himself as Alistair; the younger, skinnier man was Rab. Bea seemed willing to

accept the apology after both men promised to take
their boots off inside.

"There we go. Job done!" Alistair smiled as he stood
in his socks. "We'll be in and out a bit," he explained. "I'm
keeping an eye on the electrics outside and in the building
too. The last thing we want to do is cut a cable and have
the lights going off. We don't want a candlelit museum!"

"Imagine my job if I had to scrape wax off the floors!" exclaimed Bea, deciding that grit wasn't so bad after all.

Having won her over, Alistair and Rab departed, and the Squad rushed off, leaving the busy cleaner to fight her battle for clean surfaces. They needed to grab Mrs Gomez before the school group left the museum and vanished along with the broken-up Viking.

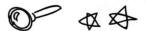

At the longship, they found Erik alone. "The schoolchildren and their scary teacher have just gone to catch their bus," he said, looking relieved.

The Squad sprinted back through the main hall and spotted Mrs Gomez at the cloakroom, handing over a bunch of tickets while her class stood patiently nearby.

The Squad waited for the perfect moment to pounce.

The cloakroom attendant handed over Mrs Gomez's bags, tubes and boxes. She passed them to pupils to carry, then used her machine-gun clap.

CLAP-CLAP-CLAP-CLAP-CLAP

"OK, children. Time for the bus back to school! Let's show those other classes who's **THE BEST!**"

"She's clever," said Kennedy. "No one would suspect a teacher with a group of schoolchildren."

"And getting the kids to carry her stolen goods – genius!" agreed Nabster.

As the class trooped out of the building, the Squad made their move.

"Excuse me, Mrs Gomez! What's inside these bags and boxes?" Laurie's question was as direct as ever.

The teacher looked surprised for a second. "Oh... It's just stuff from the museum."

She seemed quite calm about being caught. The Squad looked suspicious.

"You want to see?" Mrs Gomez bent to open a box that was the right shape and size to hold a Viking figure's head.

Nabster set down his equipment bag and removed his camera, ready to take photos of the evidence.

They all leaned in.

Inside the box was a plastic globe. It was marked with lines showing the journeys Vikings had made across oceans as they raided and settled.

"Isn't it brilliant?" said Mrs Gomez. "The museum had a spare one!"

Next up was the bulky shopping bag. Mrs Gomez opened it to reveal bundles of tunics. Kennedy poked at them – there was no body inside.

"Old Viking dressing-up clothes," explained Mrs Gomez. "The museum has new ones so they were throwing these out."

"And the arms? Er, I mean, those cardboard tubes?" asked Nabster.

"Arms?" Mrs Gomez was confused. "You mean posters! Exhibition extras. Our display will be **MAGNIFICENT!"**

Mrs Gomez had lots of the museum's stuff, but she was no Viking thief. The Squad watched, deflated, as the class headed towards their bus, Mrs Gomez leading them in a chorus of 'We Are the Champions'.

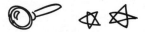

Kennedy, Nabster and Laurie walked gloomily back towards the museum, dragging their feet.

"I see what Bea means about this grit," said Laurie. His leather Viking slippers had picked up gravel from the pavement.

"I hope you're going to take your shoes off when you go back inside!" Alistair popped out of a little red-and-white road workers' tent nearby. "What do you think?" He waved a hand proudly at the newly laid paving slabs beneath their feet. Laurie and Kennedy nodded approval while Nabster watched Rab adjust wiring at the base of a brand-new streetlight.

"Nice one, Rab!" called Alistair as the light came on.

Rab gave a thumbs-up and pointed to the museum.

Alistair grinned. "And the lights are still on inside! Phew! Job done!"

"I'm glad someone's having a good day at work," said Nabster, disheartened that their vanishing Viking case had stalled.

"We need more clues," said Kennedy as they walked

back inside. "There's only one place to go. It's given us an eyeball and a coded letter, but the longship *must* hold another clue. A Viking figure can't just vanish."

It was an hour before the museum closed, and only a few last visitors wandered through the exhibitions. There was no one in the Viking Zone when the Squad arrived. Kennedy was first up the longship's ramp, but when she reached the top she suddenly stopped, putting a finger to her lips to tell the others to be quiet.

The Squad were not alone.

Chapter 6
In which sticks make words

Kennedy, Laurie and Nabster huddled at the top of

the ramp and peered into the longship. At the far

end, someone was leaning over the Viking sledge and

seemed to be handling the treasure. They were wearing

ripped jeans and a hoodie, and it was difficult to

see their face.

"Who is it?" hissed Nabster.

"And what are they doing?" murmured Laurie,

watching as the person put a brooch back on the

sledge's pile of silver.

Their whispers weren't quiet enough and the person turned, revealing not the shocked face of a guilty thief, but a broadly smiling woman with a long blonde braid.

"Hi! I wondered when we would meet," she said.

The Squad looked baffled.

"I've heard all about you," she explained, stepping forward to greet them.

It was Laurie who worked it out. "Are you Erik's twin?" he asked.

"That's me!" she replied brightly. "I'm Astrid. Not an identical twin, as you can see! But Erik and I are the same in some ways – we're both Viking through and through!"

"Are you really?" asked Laurie.

"Yes! We've had DNA tests done and traced our family tree. It goes right back to Viking times."

"That guy could be a relative!" Nabster pointed to the skeleton.

"Exactly," nodded Astrid. "This treasure is like our family jewels!"

"Erik dresses more like a Viking than you do," observed Kennedy.

"Yeah, he wears his costume the whole time," said Astrid. "I find mine a bit scratchy!"

"What does yours look like?" asked Laurie.

"Oh, nothing fancy. Just a long dress and pinafore – all handmade. The Vikings made thread from wool and wove their clothes, then they added colour by making dye from plants."

"I'd never thought about where colour comes from," said Laurie.

"Their jewellery was a bit more interesting." Astrid waved at the shiny pile of Viking treasure. "I really love the designs, especially their brooches: dragons, wolves, turtles. All sorts of creatures." She pointed to the coiled snake brooch they had seen her touching. "That one's my favourite. I was just getting ready for tomorrow's school groups and I couldn't resist a closer look. It's the same as the one I use on my costume – although mine's just a copy."

The Squad admired the brooches, then Astrid said she had to find Erik. She passed Gus coming up the longship ramp as she left.

"I've *finally* finished looking through that daytime CCTV footage," he said. "Nothing to report. They should call it 'Don't-See TV' instead of 'CCTV'... get it? 'See' (he pointed to his eyes) not 'C' (he drew a curvy letter C in the air)?"

"Yeah, we see." Kennedy grimaced at her choice of words.

"There was no sign of our vanishing friend," continued Gus. "The only Vikings walking out of the building that day were Astrid and Erik, and they were the only visitors with a big bag too."

"I guess it's full of costumes and props from their school talks," said Kennedy.

Laurie sighed wearily, leaning back against the longship's mast.

Kennedy felt like flopping too, but glancing at Laurie she immediately perked up.

"Look!" She pointed. "Behind you! It's that twig code!"

On the mast beside Laurie's head was a little information panel displaying the same shapes as the scrap of paper he'd found earlier that day.

Laurie peered at the explanation. "Apparently they're called 'runes'," he said.

"Ruins?" Nabster echoed. "Like broken buildings?"

"No!" Kennedy read the information too. "*Runes*. They're Viking writing!"

Laurie read on. "It says these symbols are part of the Viking alphabet. Each has a name and a sound. Look, there's a diagram of the symbols here and the closest matching sound in our alphabet."

ᚠ	ᚢ	ᚦ	ᚨ	ᚱ	ᚲ	ᚷ	ᚹ
f	u	th	a	r	k	g	w
ᚺ	ᚾ	ᛁ	ᛃ	ᛇ	ᛈ	ᛉ	ᛋ
h	n	i	j	ae	p	z	s
ᛏ	ᛒ	ᛖ	ᛗ	ᛚ	ᛜ	ᛞ	ᛟ
t	b	e	m	l	ng	d	o

Nabster and Kennedy crowded round.

"Sounds like Norse Code!" said Gus. "Get it? *Norse Code*... like Morse Code?... But Norse was the language of the Vikings!"

No one laughed. The Squad had something else on their minds.

"This is the key we need to decode the writing on the prankster's letter!" exclaimed Laurie.

"Time to read runes and find the vanishing Viking!" said Kennedy.

Putting his equipment bag down, Nabster took photos of the rune diagram, as well as a few snaps of the rest of the longship. Then the Squad headed to the HQ, all set to crack the prankster's code.

Chapter 7
In which something unexpected is pulled from a pocket

"Right, let's find out what 'A Bit of Viking Fun' really means," said Kennedy at the smartboard, pen in hand.

There were what looked like three sentences of symbols on the piece of paper, and Laurie and Nabster started to pick their way through the first. Using Nabster's photo of the diagram, they called out the matching letters for Kennedy to write.

Five minutes later she read the result. *"A bad rower blames the oar.* Sounds like an old Viking saying. I suppose it means if you can't do something, don't say it's because of your equipment."

"Like Laurie blaming his sleeping bag if he couldn't get to sleep!" said Nabster.

"An unlikely event," said Laurie, yawning.

"Hmm," said Kennedy thoughtfully. "But why would pranksters send old Viking sayings to each other?"

"Perhaps they have secret meanings," suggested Nabster, "like code phrases in spy films."

The second one was longer. It took them a while to match up symbols with sounds, and there seemed to be some missing letters.

"*You will reach your destination even though you travel slowly,*" read Kennedy, working it out.

"Just like this case." Laurie yawned again. "We're not moving fast but we'll get there!"

"Glad you think so." Nabster sounded doubtful.

There was a knock at the door: an unusual occurrence for the Squad HQ. The room was tucked away under the museum in such a maze of corridors that not many people found their way to it unless they were completely lost or – as in this case – they had a plan of the building.

Kennedy opened the door to reveal Alistair, the man doing the roadworks, padding around in thick woolly socks instead of dirty boots. (Bea would have been delighted that he was polishing the floors with every step.)

"I struggled to find you," he said, smiling. "Just as well I had this plan! It's supposed to be for checking the wiring." He waved his roll of paper.

"Does that map really have this room on it?" asked Nabster, keen to see their hidden headquarters on a plan.

"Of course – it shows every nook and cranny of the museum," said Alistair. "But you might be *more* interested in something else I've brought – something I think you've lost."

"The Viking?" shouted all three Squad members at once.

"Viking? No... something much smaller. Gus told me this guy belongs to you." Alistair lifted a familiar friend from his jacket pocket.

"COLIN!"

"I didn't even realise he was missing," confessed Nabster. "I thought he was still asleep in my bag."

"Well, he obviously likes an adventure. I found him outside!" reported Alistair.

"How did he get there?" asked Laurie, amazed.

Nabster looked thoughtful. "I put my bag on the ground when we stopped Mrs Gomez. He must have climbed out."

"Well, he's back where he belongs," said Alistair. "Job done!" He opened his plan again. "Now... how do I get out of here? The museum's about to close."

Kennedy walked with him to the end of the corridor and gave him a complicated set of directions.

"I wish I *had* left a trail of gritty footprints!" he muttered, padding away in his socks.

Nabster put Colin safely back in his cage. "What are you like, Colin? Did you see the big wide world? Spot any missing Vikings?"

If Colin had, then he didn't give any clues. He was just happy to be home, especially since Gus had taken away the berserker.

The next morning, Colin was woken from a carrot-induced slumber by excited muttering. Kennedy was standing at the smartboard, holding the torn page of runes.

"We forgot about the final rune last night when Alistair brought Colin back!" she said. "I've just worked it out. There's a bit missing, but we've got the start. And look what it says!"

Laurie and Nabster stared up at the decoded message.

"FIND AND TAKE..." Nabster read aloud.

Laurie sprang up from the sofa. "Hang on, 'find and take'? That *has* to be about pranksters stealing the Viking, doesn't it?"

"Maybe they couldn't be seen together, so these sayings were how they communicated their plan," said Nabster.

"We *need* to find the rest of that paper," said Kennedy. "This saying might tell us where the Viking vanished to."

But before the Squad could plan their search, they were interrupted by the walkie-talkie crackling into life.

"Gus calling the Squad. Are you receiving? Over."

The tone of his voice sounded urgent.

"Go ahead, Gus. Over."

"You're needed. Viking Zone. Now. Over."

"On our way. What's up? Over."

"Something else has vanished. This time it's valuable. Come quickly. Over and out."

RUNE DECODING

Vikings often carved scary names in runes on their weapons, as they believed it made them more powerful in battle. Can you use the key to help Nabster decode the names opposite? Check the answers at the back of the book to see if you're right.

ᚠ	ᚢ	ᚦ	ᚨ	ᚱ	ᚲ	ᚷ	ᚹ
f	u	th	a	r	k	g	w

ᚺ	ᚾ	ᛁ	ᛃ	ᛇ	ᛈ	ᛉ	ᛋ
h	n	i	j	ae	p	z	s

ᛏ	ᛒ	ᛖ	ᛗ	ᛚ	ᛜ	ᛞ	ᛟ
t	b	e	m	l	ng	d	o

DID YOU KNOW...

The Viking alphabet was called *futhark*, named after the first six runic character sounds. Runes were more than just letters, they had meanings too, for example the rune 'ᚠ' meant 'wealth'.

EXAMPLE:

ᛋᚲᚢᛚᛚ ᛋᚲᛚᛁᛏᛏᛗᚱ = SKULL SPLITTER

1. ᛚᛗᚷ ᛒᚱᛗᚨᚲᛗᚱ = Leg breaker

2. ᚠᚱᛗᚨᚾᚱ ᚱᛁᚲᚲᛗᚱ = Armour ripper

3. ᚠᛚᛗᛋᚾ ᛋᛏᛁᚾᚷᛗᚱ = Flesh stinger

4. ᛒᚨᚾᛗ ᛋᛗᚨᛋᚾᛗᚱ = Bone smasher

5. ᛋᚾᛁᛗᛚᚨ ᛋᚲᛚᛁᛏᛏᛗᚱ = shield splitter

Make up your own Viking weapon name and write it in runes below. Careful though, our alphabet has some letters the runic alphabet doesn't!

ᛒᛚᛄᛄᚾ ᛒᚱᛗᚨᚲᛗᚱ

blood   breaker

ANSWERS
ON THE
LAST
PAGE

Chapter 8
In which there are tattoos worth looking at

"This is *very* serious," said Magda Gaskar. "The Viking figure vanishing was strange and inconvenient, but this is the theft of rare and precious items."

The Squad, Gus and Magda stood inside the longship looking at another space. The sledge was empty. The treasure that had been piled on it was gone. Missing. Vanished.

Gus and Magda left to report the theft to the police. Nabster set to work, getting down on his hands and knees with a magnifying glass, just as Erik and Astrid strode on board the longship.

"We heard about the jewels!" said Astrid breathlessly. "It's so sad!"

She was wearing her Viking costume: a long pinafore under an animal-skin cloak, which was held in place by a large brooch with a coiled snake design. On her back she carried a colourful wooden shield.

Erik explained they were expecting a new school group, so the Squad had to be quick with their search.

They looked around quickly, but uncovered no clues to show how the treasure had been stolen, and no missing piece of the rune message.

"The only thing I've found is more of the grit that annoys Bea so much," said Nabster.

"She did say it gets everywhere," replied Kennedy.

"Yeah. It's bit odd though," said Nabster. "It just seems to be near the sledge." His eye looked enormous as he peered through the magnifying glass. "There's none anywhere else on the longship, or in the rest of the Zone. Surely there should be a trail of it across the deck and into the museum?"

"So now we even have missing grit!" said Kennedy. "Look, the new school group is arriving. We need to discuss the vanishing treasure: back to the HQ!"

Kennedy's Diary

Friday 11 a.m.

This case feels like the strangest magic trick ever! A Viking figure, a heap of treasure and a trail of grit have all disappeared. Can we figure out what's going on?

- No Viking seen or filmed on CCTV leaving the room — how did it get out?

- No *body* found apart from an eyeball — where's the rest of it?

- A coded letter in runes, but half of it is missing — who wrote it?

- Treasure there one day and gone the next — how's that possible?

- Grit near the sledge but nowhere else — why?

So many questions... it's time for answers.

There was a new sense of purpose among the Museum Mystery Squad. The theft of the treasure had changed the case entirely.

"I don't think the vanishing Viking figure was a prank after all – it must be connected to the stolen treasure," reasoned Kennedy.

"At least this time the answer to 'Why would someone take this?' is obvious," said Laurie. "The treasure is worth a fortune."

"It's the 'How?' that bothers me." Nabster looked thoughtful. "How can a heap of treasure just disappear? Gus says last night's CCTV shows nothing leaving the Zone."

"What about the 'Who?'" asked Kennedy. "Who would want treasure and jewellery?"

"Laurie!" answered Nabster.

Laurie held his hands up. "True, but not guilty."

Nabster scrolled through his photos. Images flashed across the smartboard: the longship, colourful shields, the sledge, runes, weapons, brooches.

"STOP!" shouted Kennedy.

"What, what, what?" Nabster's fingers froze in mid-air.

"We know someone else who likes jewellery," said Kennedy. The screen was filled with a close-up picture of the sledge and treasure from the previous day. It showed the Viking brooch decorated with a coiled snake.

"Astrid!" cried Laurie. "When we first met her she was touching the treasure..."

"She said that brooch was her favourite," remembered Kennedy.

"And she called the treasure 'the family jewels'," said Nabster. "Does she think it should be hers because it belonged to her ancestors?"

"Maybe we interrupted her last night," suggested Laurie, "then she went back to finish the job?"

"She could have had some help."

"From who?"

"A twin brother?"

"Could Erik and Astrid be in this together?"

Nabster flicked through the images, looking for a picture of the twins.

Laurie was frowning inside his Viking helmet. "They always wear jewellery. They could put on the treasure and walk out the door, and no one would even notice! What if the brooch we just saw Astrid wearing *isn't* her costume – what if it's the real one?!"

"After the Viking vanished, Gus said he saw Erik and Astrid on CCTV leaving the museum with their big bag," said Kennedy. "It would have been easy to hide pieces of the figure among their props."

Nabster had found an image of Astrid and Erik. Erik's lower arm was covered in jewellery, his tattoos peeking out between stacks of bracelets.

"Hey, look at that!" Kennedy had noticed something. "Some of his tattoos are words in runes!"

"I wonder what they say?" pondered Laurie.

"Probably **I LOVE VIKINGS**,"

grumbled Nabster, who was getting tired of rune solving. But he enlarged the image, and Laurie called out letters while Kennedy wrote them on the smartboard underneath the photo.

"This looks familiar," she said. "F...I...N...D... A...N...D... T...A...K...E... The tattoo is the same as the saying from the torn letter!"

"Well, there's more on the tattoo," said Nabster reading on.

F...I...N...D... A...N...D... T...A...K...E... T...H...E... T...R...

"Oh my word!" cried Kennedy as the decoded message emerged.

They all looked in silence, struggling to believe it.

"*Find and take the treasure,*" Laurie read.

"This is it!" Kennedy punched the air in excitement. "They're claiming it back. Erik has a tattoo on his arm about *taking* treasure!"

"The Vikings are raiding the museum..." said Nabster. "For their ancestors' treasure!"

Laurie picked up the torn page of runes he had found the day before. "I bet this is a coded letter between the twins."

Nabster grabbed the walkie-talkie. It was time for action. "Nabster calling Gus. Receiving? Over."

"Gus here. Please tell me nothing else has vanished. Over."

Nabster spoke quickly. "Can you locate Erik or Astrid? Over."

"Yes. Erik was outside the gift shop two minutes ago. No sign of Astrid. Over."

"How did Erik look? Over."

There was a pause.

"Same as usual. Like a Viking. Helmet. Cloak. Fancy brooch. Loads of bracelets and a medallion or two. Carrying a bag. Over."

"Thanks, Gus. Over and out."

Nabster turned to Laurie and Kennedy. "Right. We need to tackle a thief who is also a very big Viking. Any idea how we do that?"

"Easy," said Kennedy, sprinting for the door.

WHICH NORSE DEITY ARE YOU?

The Vikings worshipped lots of gods and goddesses, known as deities, who each had their own special qualities. Take the quiz below to find out if you're more of a troublesome trickster like Loki, or a wise leader like Odin.

1. How would your friends describe you?
a. Brave
b. Wise
c. Caring
d. Mischievous

2. Your favourite day of the week is...?
a. Thursday
b. Wednesday
c. Friday
d. Sunday

3. What do you like to do in your spare time?
a. Battle your enemies on computer games
b. Watch TV
c. Read
d. Play pranks on your friends and family

4. Your idea of a perfect holiday is...?
a. An activity holiday — the more extreme sports the better!
b. Somewhere with lots of museums — knowledge is power
c. Anywhere — as long as it's with friends and family
d. Having fun in the pool — you love splashing people!

5. Your teacher would say you...
a. Stand up for your friends
b. Are a real leader
c. Are always top of the class
d. Get into trouble. A lot!

6. Your dream pet would be...?
a. A dog
b. A horse
c. An owl
d. A snake

ANSWERS ON THE LAST PAGE

Chapter 9
In which there are different kinds of treasure

If there was ever an example of Kennedy's fearlessness, this was it. Nabster and Laurie were nervous about challenging Erik, but Kennedy didn't hesitate. She spotted him lumbering through the museum's entrance hall, marched alongside, then swerved in front of him so sharply that he nearly tripped over.

"Whoops!" said the giant man. "You're a small girl in a big hurry!"

Kennedy pulled herself up to her full height (about

half Erik's size) and took a deep breath.

"I've got a question for you," she announced.

"OK..." Erik looked uncertain.

Laurie and Nabster stood behind Kennedy, who went on, "One of your tattoos reads: *Find and take the treasure*!" She pointed. "And we are investigating missing Viking treasure."

"Wow! You guys are good at rune solving!" Erik replied. He began pulling bracelets off his wrist.

"And do you recognise *this*?" Laurie held up the torn sheet of paper with the runes on it.

"Yes, I do," replied Astrid, strolling up behind Erik and reaching into their bag. "We've got 120 copies right here." She held up a familiar-looking list of runes but on an untorn sheet of paper. The Squad saw the full heading:

Rune Solving Activity Sheet –
A Bit of Viking Fun.

It was a set of puzzles for school pupils, not a secret coded letter.

Erik held out his arm for the Squad.

"Here, you are right, it says *Find and take the treasure.*" Then he slipped the last arm band off over his hand. "And here is the rest," he said.

The rune tattoo continued. It had been half hidden by Erik's bracelets.

"What does that bit mean?" asked Laurie.

"We can work it out," said Nabster.

He made some quick notes before looking up. "I think the rest of it reads: *in life.*"

"Find and take the treasure in life," repeated Kennedy slowly.

"Inspiring, isn't it?" said Erik. "It reminds me to look for the good things in the world. Life's real treasures are kind people and special moments. We must remember to find and appreciate them."

Kennedy sighed, but Nabster wasn't quite ready to give up. He turned to Astrid. "Can I see your brooch?" His Scanray might still prove their theory that the stolen treasure was being worn under everyone's noses.

"Sure!" Astrid unclipped the pin behind the coiled snake.

The Scanray hummed. Its screen said:

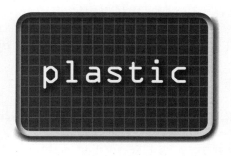

Kennedy's Diary

Friday 1 p.m.

It wasn't pranksters, it wasn't Mrs Gomez, and it wasn't Erik and Astrid. We've apologised for accusing the twins, but we've still got a vanished Viking and missing treasure to find.

I'm starting to wish this whole case would just disappear!

All was quiet in the Squad HQ. There was no evidence being discussed, no ideas being suggested, no action being taken. But everyone was thinking about the case in their own way.

Kennedy was writing in her diary.

Laurie looked like he was asleep, but his mind was busy trying to make sense of what they'd learned.

Nabster was checking measurements he'd made and photos he'd taken, hoping a tiny clue might jump out. He flashed through his images, zooming in close on swords and axes, the longship's dragon figurehead, the sledge, and...

"COLIN?!"

In his cage the hamster recognised his name and poked his head out of the straw.

"How come I've got a photo of Colin?" Nabster looked confused and quickly enlarged the image.

There was Colin, in front of the sledge, inside the longship. He was only a tiny figure, but it was definitely him.

Kennedy and Laurie both looked up.

"I put Colin in my bag here in the HQ," said Nabster, thinking it through. "Then we went upstairs and outside and accused Mrs Gomez, then saw Alistair, then we came back in and found Astrid in the longship."

Kennedy nodded. "Alistair brought him back to us because he'd escaped when we were out on the street tackling Mrs Gomez."

"But look!" Nabster zoomed in further. There was no mistaking Colin's furry head, or the fact he was on the longship.

"That's actually a very funny photo." Laurie laughed.

"It looks like he's taken a bad selfie!"

"But see, if Colin is in this picture," said Nabster, "it means he didn't disappear when we were outside the museum. He was still with us when we met Astrid and I took these photos."

"Hang on, Alistair found him outside," said Laurie. "How did he get there from the Viking Zone?"

"An incredible journey through the museum?" Kennedy sounded unconvinced.

"But he'd have to have scampered across the big main hall and opened doors." Laurie was also doubtful.

As Laurie and Kennedy looked puzzled, Nabster smiled.

"Of course!" he said. "This *is* like a magician's vanishing trick! Magic is about illusions. Like using secret compartments or trapdoors that open to make things disappear. We need to get back to the longship – and Colin needs to come too!"

Colin didn't complain at being plucked from his cage again. A straw-filled pocket in Nabster's bag was a comfortable way to travel. "I've got a special way of keeping a close eye on you this time!" Nabster said. He pulled a small black object from his pocket before attaching it to a length of string from his bag and slipping the makeshift collar gently over the hamster's head.

"Right, Colin. It's time for you to show us your disappearing trick," said Nabster as they arrived at the 'Raiders, Traders and Settlers' display. "I have a hunch the Viking Zone has a secret. There must be a hidden exit we don't know about..."

He lifted Colin out of the bag – and the hamster squeaked his loudest squeak, squeezed through Nabster's fingers onto the floor, and was off like a shot!

"What's got into him?" asked Laurie.

"That guy!" Kennedy pointed. Unfortunately Colin had spotted the shield-biting berserker, and he wasn't happy.

"Where's he gone?"

They got a glimpse of Colin speeding past furs and swords and scales.

"Up the ramp!"

They charged onto the longship chasing the brown-and-white furry blur, but when they arrived amongst the sea chests and skull-splitters there was no sign of Colin.

"Gone!" Laurie looked worried.

"Don't worry," said Nabster. He pulled out a screen. "This time I've put my tracker on Colin's DIY collar. Nothing vanishes when this is involved!"

Sure enough, the little screen showed a flashing dot.

"He's not far away." Nabster moved slowly through the longship to locate the missing hamster.

The search took them towards the spot where the Viking had once stood and where the sledge now sat empty. Looking closer, they spotted a crack across some of the longship's timbers.

Kennedy knelt down. "Do you have a screwdriver?"

"Of course!" said Nabster, producing his favourite one triumphantly. "It's the one missing thing that *has* been found."

120

"If I put it in here," said Kennedy, sliding it into the gap, "and pull up..."

"Are you out of your mind?!" Laurie cried.

Kennedy held up a big panel from the bottom of the ship.

Laurie continued to panic. "Magda will kill us! Then stuff us! Then put us on display!"

A little furry head popped up from a hole below, sniffing the air.

"Colin!"

Nabster lifted out his hamster friend, checking him over before carefully putting him back into the bag pocket.

He put away the tracker screen then pulled out a torch and shone it into the hole. Under the longship's flat hull was a dark opening in the museum floor.

"Why is there a hole here?" Laurie's curiosity had got the better of him.

"Not sure." Nabster peered in. "But there's a ladder into a long tunnel."

"There's only one thing for it," said Kennedy. "If Colin can do it, so can we. We're going in!"

Chapter 10
In which there is bubble wrap

It was a tight fit as Kennedy, Nabster and Laurie eased themselves through the hole and down the short ladder. Everything went dark for a few seconds while their eyes adjusted to the gloom.

"What is this place?" Laurie's voice echoed.

Nabster's torch showed that they had gone right through the longship floor and into a tunnel that was lined with old bricks.

Nabster looked around, trying to get his bearings. "Some kind of old maintenance access under the museum's display rooms. It's underground, but I think it's above the corridors we use to get to the HQ."

"It feels really old," said Laurie.

Nabster sniffed. "Smells that way too."

"Look! There's a date," said Kennedy.

The light from the torch picked out one of the bricks, engraved with a year.

"The year the museum was built."

"It goes on for ages." Nabster's torch showed the passageway stretching into the distance.

"Let's see where it takes us," said Kennedy bravely, but also sounding a bit nervous. "Put the panel back in place so we haven't left a big hole in the longship."

"Er... OK," replied Laurie, feeling a lot less brave and an awful lot more nervous. He replaced the square of wood.

Suddenly Nabster gasped, his torch falling to the floor. The light clicked off. They were plunged into complete darkness.

"What's wrong?" asked Kennedy.

"There's someone here!" whispered Nabster.

"Where?" hissed Kennedy.

"Lying on the ground!" Nabster scrabbled to find his torch.

"I don't like this," whimpered Laurie. "I don't like this at all."

Nabster switched the torch back on and shone it along the passageway to reveal a large shape lying on the floor in front of them. It was a man.

"Is he moving?" asked Laurie, hiding behind the others.

"No – he's got no legs!" replied Nabster.

"He has," said Kennedy. "They're just here, beside his body."

"What are you talking about?" Laurie plucked up the courage to peer between his friends. "Oh… it's a Viking!"

"Not just *any* Viking," said Nabster. "It's *the* Viking. We've found the vanishing Viking!"

The torch's beam shone on the face of the broken Viking figure. Dressed in a tunic, the life-size model of a bearded warrior stared back at them. With one eye. His axe lay alongside him. As did his legs.

Nabster moved the torch around. "It looks like he's had a bit of an accident!"

"Exactly," said Kennedy. "Imagine the panel I lifted being pushed open from below. It was right under the Viking, so the figure would have fallen forwards and broken. I'm guessing whoever did it couldn't fix him and decided not to leave a busted Viking lying around. They hid him down here instead."

"That's how he vanished into thin air!" said Laurie. "He didn't leave the museum and he wasn't in another Zone. There never was a prank or a theft. He disappeared through a hole and has been here under our feet the whole time!"

Nabster continued to shine the torch around. "This brick floor is gritty. Remember when the treasure went missing there was grit in the longship but not anywhere else? It must have come from here.

Someone walked along this tunnel, went up into the longship for the treasure, then came back down again without walking anywhere else in the Viking Zone."

"So where does this lead?" Laurie peered into the darkness, shivering in the cold underground air.

"There's only one way to find out," said Kennedy, striding off. "Come on."

Silenced by the darkness, they walked on tiptoes. The brick corridor twisted one way then the other.

"There's something up ahead," whispered Nabster. They'd reached a kind of crossroads, where three other tunnels led off. Shining the torch as steadily as he could, Nabster revealed a mystery object sitting at the junction: a wooden crate.

The Squad approached cautiously.

"Can I get that screwdriver again?" asked Kennedy. Seconds later she was prising the top off the crate.

They all held their breath and peered in.

"Bubble wrap," said Laurie, relaxing a bit.

"I love this stuff." Nabster took off his bag and reached into the big wooden box to softly pop some of the little air pockets.

Kennedy went further. She pulled the top sheet of bubble wrap to one side.

They all gasped.

Nestled in the crate, and protected by layers of wrapping, was the Viking treasure: bracelets, brooches, rings, coins and sharp-edged swords.

"The thieves must be planning to collect this crate soon." Kennedy was thinking hard. "We need to stop them before this treasure really vanishes."

"We should get help." Nabster tried the walkie-talkie, but there was no signal in the tunnel.

"Why don't I go back to the longship and call Gus?"

suggested Laurie. "You two wait here." He looked into the darkness behind them and gulped.

Nabster rummaged in his bag and pulled out a keyring with a tiny light. "It's not much, but it'll help."

With the light and the walkie-talkie, Laurie disappeared into the gloom. Kennedy and Nabster replaced the crate's lid.

Then a voice echoed from round the next bend in the tunnel: "Hey, did you see a light?" it asked.

Someone was coming.

The question threw Kennedy and Nabster into a panic.

"Torch off!" Kennedy whispered urgently.

Nabster flicked the switch, and they dived into the dark shadows of a branching passageway with seconds to spare. They squeezed as close to the wall as possible and held their breath, desperate not to make a noise.

133

Two beams of light appeared and two pairs of footsteps crunched on the gritty floor, followed by a loud rattling noise that echoed off the walls. The mystery intruders were wheeling something over the floor.

"I can't see anything," said one voice.

"Must have imagined it," said another.

Kennedy and Nabster froze. There was something familiar about the voices, but they couldn't risk sneaking a peek.

"Record this," whispered Kennedy in Nabster's ear.

As quietly as he could, Nabster reached down for his bag. Then stopped. He stifled a gasp.

Kennedy put her hand to her mouth. Even in the darkness, she too could see Nabster's bag on the floor beside the crate. It was seconds away from being discovered.

"Right," said one of the voices, "let's get the crate onto the trolley and wheel it along till we're under the road. Then we'll collect it in the truck tonight. Job done."

Nabster and Kennedy looked at each other. 'Job done!' Who always said that?

Alistair.

"Is this your bag?" asked the other voice. It had to be Rab.

Two beams of light lit up Nabster's bag. A skinny hand reached down and picked it up.

"Not mine."

"Well, if it's not yours, and it's not mine, that means someone else has been here!"

At that moment there was a squeal from Rab. "Ah, it's alive! Something's in it!"

He dropped the bag. For a split second, caught in

the glare of Rab's headtorch, Kennedy and Nabster saw Colin poking his head out of the side pocket.

"It's that stupid hamster," snarled Alistair. "Squash it!"

Rab lifted his heavy work boot to stamp on the bag when he was interrupted by a loud rattling noise and a blood-curdling warrior cry.

"ROOOAARRRR!"

The two men spun round to be met by a huge figure. Out of the tunnel's darkness lurched the vanishing Viking! It was moving at speed, its arm raised, battle-axe ready. Kennedy and Nabster shrank into the wall. The one-eyed warrior hurtled towards them, looking terrifying – but as it passed, they spotted a familiar bow tie. Beneath the top half of the broken figure, holding it high, was a roaring Laurie.

"ROOOAARRRR!" he screamed. "Give me my treasure!"

There were shouts as Alistair and Rab turned in fright, bumping into each other as they fled.

"How is that thing moving?!" Rab cried.

"Never mind that..." replied Alistair. "Run!"

Laurie chased after them, shouting **"GIVE ME MY TREASURE!"**

Nabster dashed over to his bag. "You were brilliant, Colin!" he said.

Kennedy rushed back towards the longship. Nabster followed with Colin.

"We'll get Gus," puffed Kennedy as they ran. "Laurie can't have got that far. We need help – quickly!"

"If they find out that Viking is actually Laurie, he could be in real trouble," agreed Nabster, his bag firmly back on his shoulder with Colin safe inside. They pushed on the wooden panel and popped their heads through the longship floor, emerging into a group of shocked-looking schoolchildren.

"Hey, you two... What's going on?" asked Erik.

"Treasure!" wheezed Nabster. "We found it! Must... catch... road workers..."

Sprinting out of the Viking Zone, Kennedy almost collided with Gus in the doorway.

"I got a strange crackly message from Laurie on the walkie-talkie," said Gus. "Something about treasure, and a tunnel?"

"Outside. Now!" cried Kennedy, pelting past him.

Before Gus could crack a joke, Nabster sped out of the

Viking Zone in hot pursuit. Gus followed them both out

of the main museum doors into the street.

Chapter 11
In which there is a Viking frisbee

Pedestrians turned to watch, mouths open in shock, as a ginger-haired girl burst from the museum's front door and skidded to a stop. A boy followed seconds later carrying a bag with a furry head popping out of a side pocket. Striding close behind was a lanky security guard.

"There!" shouted Kennedy, pointing down the street. Two men tumbled out of the little road workers' tent on the pavement, picked themselves up and, not hearing her, ran in Kennedy's direction.

"Stop them!" she cried.

Passers-by seemed confused about who they were supposed to be stopping, but one person was quick off the mark. Erik had followed the sprinting Squad members out of the museum and immediately saw what was needed. Broadening his huge shoulders and spreading his thick arms wide, he stood in the way of the escaping thieves.

"Woah, woah, woah... You're in a terrible hurry," he said with a grin. "Slow down or you'll knock someone over."

Unfortunately, that's exactly what they did. The two men ran right through him, bowling him clean off his feet.

They might have escaped if another Viking hadn't appeared. Astrid was right behind Erik. She quickly unclipped the large shield from her back and, with a Viking battle cry, threw the wooden disc like a giant Frisbee after the two crooks.

Alistair and Rab didn't know what had hit them. The shield whacked into their ankles, knocking them over like neon skittles.

"What a shot!" Nabster was seriously impressed.

Kennedy clapped with excitement. "I want her to show me how to do that – right now!"

"Looks like I need to have a word with these two," said Gus. Alistair and Rab were tangled on the ground, clutching bruised legs.

Astrid grinned and collected the shield, tucking it onto her back. She pulled Erik to his feet. "Are you sure you're really descended from Vikings?" she said with a smile.

Erik looked embarrassed. "I think they caught me off balance."

In the distance Laurie's face appeared out of the road workers' tent. "Did I miss anything?"

"Job done!" called Kennedy, grinning.

A short while later, the Squad stood on the museum steps and watched as the Viking treasure thieves were driven away in a police car. With them on the steps was Bea, looking satisfied. "I hope they've taken their mucky boots with them!" she stated firmly.

Kennedy, Nabster, Laurie and Colin returned to the Viking Zone. Magda had asked to meet them there, along with Gus, Erik and Astrid, to get a full explanation of the Case of the Vanishing Viking. Colin came too, since he'd played such an important part in solving the disappearances.

Kennedy, Nabster and Laurie showed Magda the panel in the flat bottom of the longship, and the old tunnel with the road workers' tent outside.

"The museum has a number of these tunnels," said Magda. "This old building's full of surprises."

"Alistair knew about them," said Kennedy. "His maps showed all the passageways, helping him find a sneaky way of getting into the Viking Zone. He must have worked out that the treasure was the most valuable thing he could get close to."

"Well, I'm just glad the treasure – and our vanishing Viking – have been found. Now that we've found him, we'll make sure he's put back on display in one piece," said Magda. "And we'll close up the

146

longship's hidden passageway."

"No more longship adventures for you, Colin," said Laurie with a smile.

"Colin was the star of the show." Nabster gave the little hamster an extra-large piece of carrot. "He got all the way outside by going through the tunnel. It was his disappearing trick that led us underground!"

"Well, I guess that's the *hole* story," said Gus. "Get it...? Whole story...?"

As usual after one of Gus's jokes, everything went quiet, until Erik finally spoke. "Ah... I think I get it. You are saying 'the whole story' meaning everything in the story, but you are also saying 'the hole story' because it is a story about a hole.

Very funny. That is a good one! You are a funny man!"

He patted Gus on the shoulder, nearly knocking

him over.

   For once everyone else actually did start to laugh.

Last chapter
In which the case is closed

"There's something odd about this case," said Kennedy, sitting at the table in the Squad HQ. "Maybe it's because the Vikings were great travellers, but this mystery contained loads of unusual things that were on the move."

"What do you mean?" asked Nabster, sliding the three magician's cups around on the tabletop very fast.

"First the Viking figure moved," said Kennedy.

"Well, that was certainly unusual," agreed Nabster. "Especially since it left an eyeball behind."

"Then there was Colin," continued Kennedy. "He doesn't normally travel, but he covered a *lot* of ground in this case!"

"True." Nabster nodded.

"But the biggest surprise of all..." said Kennedy. "Did you see the speed Laurie moved at when he was pretending to be a Viking?"

"Unbelievable," Nabster laughed. "Now that *must* have been magic!"

"Ha ha," came a voice from the sofa. Laurie snuggled into his sleeping bag. "I think I'd make a very good Viking. Forget the raiding and trading, I'm *the* expert at settling. Goodnight."

"And I'm determined to become an expert at this trick," said Nabster. "Right... which cup is the ball under?"

Kennedy reached out a hand, then realised she wasn't so sure this time. She thought for a bit and tapped the left-hand cup. Nabster lifted it. There was nothing beneath.

"Wahey!" he shouted. "I've done it!"

"So where is it?" asked Kennedy. She turned the other two cups over.

The ball was nowhere to be seen.

"Um..." Nabster looked confused. "I'm not actually sure." He started looking around the table and then underneath on the floor. "It's really vanished!"

"We could get Colin on the case," suggested Kennedy.

But there wasn't much chance of that. Colin was curled up in his straw. Although he was sleeping, he was still having adventures. He was dreaming of sailing in a longship carved from an enormous carrot, completely unaware that the missing magic ball was hidden in the corner of his cage.

Mike Nicholson

Mike Phillips

Mike Nicholson is a bike rider, shortbread baker, bad juggler and ear wiggler, and author of the *Museum Mystery Squad* series among other books for children.

Mike Phillips learnt to draw by copying characters from his favourite comics. Now he spends his days drawing astronauts, pirates, crocodiles and other cool things.

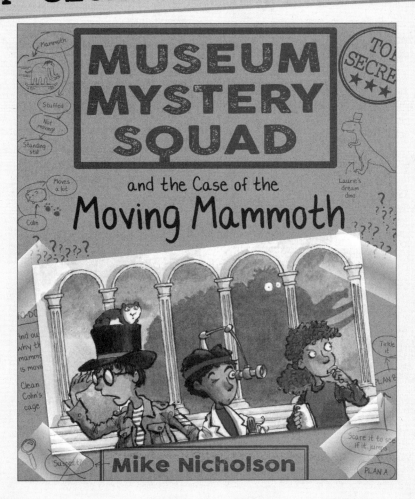

How can an extinct mammoth be moving at night? And what do stuffed animals and a dinosaur circus have to do with it?

VIKING WORDSEARCH

The vanishing Viking isn't the only thing the Squad can't find. Can you help them uncover these hidden words? Answers at the back of the book.

LONGSHIP   RAIDERS   RUNES

BERSERKER   TRADERS   SHIELD

HOARD   SETTLERS   AXE

NORSE   ODIN   WARRIOR

THOR   HELMET   LOKI

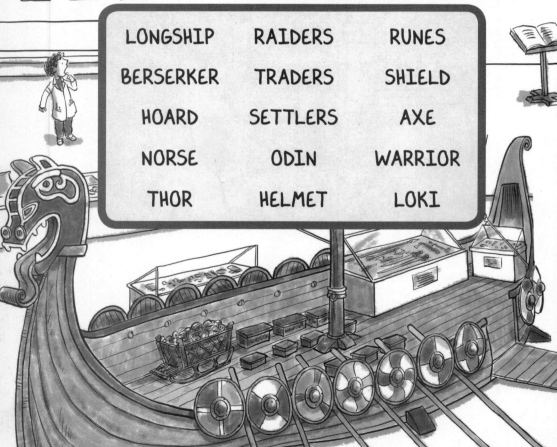

T	R	A	I	D	E	R	S	D	L
E	H	P	X	M	B	G	L	O	N
T	R	A	D	E	E	T	K	H	R
L	H	E	N	M	R	I	M	O	U
E	L	O	N	G	S	H	I	P	N
R	A	D	R	K	E	O	I	N	S
S	T	N	O	O	R	R	L	S	E
R	R	I	E	L	K	D	D	E	T
O	A	H	S	H	E	L	M	E	T
I	D	A	R	E	R	O	A	H	L
R	E	I	O	U	H	N	F	U	E
R	R	A	N	I	L	O	N	G	R
A	S	E	N	T	P	R	A	X	S
W	S	D	L	E	I	H	S	R	H
B	E	R	S	B	A	S	M	E	D

VIKING FUNNIES

Gus has lots of Viking jokes to share with the Squad. Here are some of his ~~worst~~ best one-liners...

What's a Viking warrior's favourite kind of fish?

Swordfish.

How did the Viking get his arm cut off?

It was an **axe**-ident.

What kind of songs do baby Vikings like?

Norse-ry rhymes.

How do Viking spies send secret messages?

Norse code.

What happens when a red longship crashes into a blue longship?

The crew get **marooned**.

What do you call a vegetarian Viking?

Norvegan.

Why did the Viking go to hospital?
Because he had a **Thor** thumb.

Why did the Viking throw away his broken sword?
Because it was **rune**-d.

Why couldn't the Viking play cards?
He was sitting on the **deck**.

Why did the Viking cross the ocean?
To get to the other **tide**.

Why do Vikings find the alphabet so difficult?
They get lost at **C**.

WHICH NORSE DEITY ARE YOU?
(Page 106)

Mostly A's – you're Thor!

The sky god of war and thunder, Thor was loyal and brave, just like you! He used his magical hammer called *mjölnir* in battle – this is how Vikings believed thunder and lightning were made!

Mostly B's – you're Odin!

Just like Odin, you're full of wisdom. The leader of all of the gods, Odin was worshipped for his knowledge and power. Vikings believed he watched humans from his throne in Asgard (where the gods lived), and that he rode an eight-legged horse called *Sleipnir.*

Mostly C's – you're Frigg!

Clever and caring, you're just like Frigg. The goddess of wisdom and love, she was also known for her clever plans and could see into the future using her magical powers!

Mostly D's – you're Loki!

Like Loki, you're a real trickster and love nothing more than playing a prank or two! The son of a frost giant, Loki wasn't really a god, but he was famous for shapeshifting and causing lots of mischief.

VIKING WORDSEARCH
(Page 156)

```
T R A I D E R S D L
E H P X M B G L O N
T R A D E E T K H R
L H E N M R I M O U
E L O N G S H I P N
R A D R K E O I N S
S T N O O R R L S E
R R I E L K D D E T
O A H S H E L M E T
I D A R E R O A H L
R E I O U H N F U E
R R A N I L O N G R
A S E N T P R A X S
W S D L E I H S R H
B E R S B A S M E D
```

RUNE DECODING
(Page 92)

1. Leg breaker
2. Armour ripper
3. Flesh stinger
4. Bone smasher
5. Shield splitter